CONQUERING THE UNNATURAL

HELLO!

This story is work of imagination. With the blend of magic, ghosts and Haunted House. The story is work of an adventure ride of a ten-year-old boy, who happens to be the central character of the story.

The story revolves around a Haunted House. So, fasten your belt for a haunted house ride. With lots of twists and turns at the end it is a hunky dory ride. Have fun.

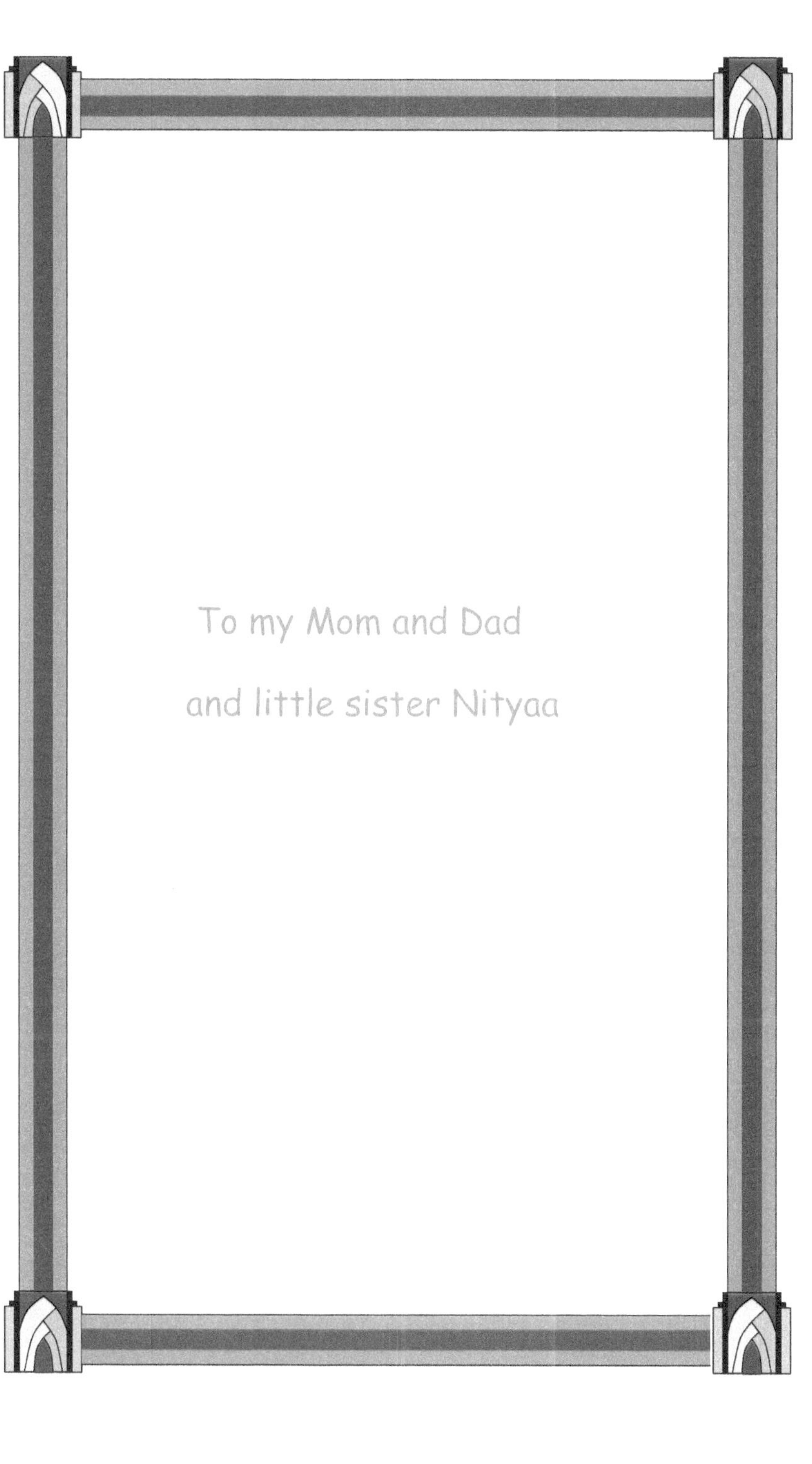

To my Mom and Dad
and little sister Nityaa

Acknowledgement

I sincerely thank Mother Universe, God for providing me the resources and my mother, Preeti Kewlani for pushing me to do this book because, I totally gave up in between but my mother stood by me like a rock.

I sincerely thank my family, for inspiring me and standing by my side for writing this book. I was given a free chance by my parents to pursue this story, which is close to my imagination.

I would urge every parent to let their child explore their imagination.

I hope I can entertain you and keep you glued till the end.

Stay tuned for the next stories too.

Happy Reading!!

With Gratitude,

Yohaan

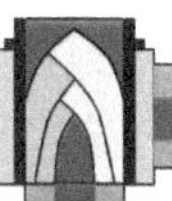

About the author

Yohaan Meghani is an avid reader and writer. Since childhood he has worked on several stories with his mother. He is very fond of playing guitar, reading books apart from Cricket and football.

Inspired by his mother's YouTube channel Preeti Kewlani, he started, his YouTube channel **Yobro Gamerz**. He loves to play chess with mom and tease his sister Nityaa.

His mother is a Chartered Accountant and Registered Valuer, he also gets inspired to be a number wizard.

Chapter 1   -The White Ghosts and Zombies

It was a shiny sunny day Yohaan was walking with his backpack, he suddenly observed that the wind started blowing fast, the trees were shaking and started making noise. Yohaan was walking, he fell into a tunnel he found himself in a strange place then he removed a torch from his backpack, turned it on and started to see what there is.

Yohaan had packed some food and other stuff and now he will solve the mystery of the haunted house. He switched on the torch and was gazing at everything around him. He saw something suspicious and was willing to walk with a thumping heartbeat and he was taken aback with what he saw a white ghost and he tried to run to escape away.

Then he saw many ghosts and once he had put the torch light on one of the ghosts and the ghost was scared of the light.

Now he knows that white ghosts are afraid of torch light. He, is observing the haunted house, then he thought that someone is following him so he looked at his back and saw a zombie he ran as fast as he could. Then he saw that with that zombie a whole bunch of zombies were following him. The white ghosts came again. He saw one broken door and hid behind it, the zombies thought that he ran far away so they went back.

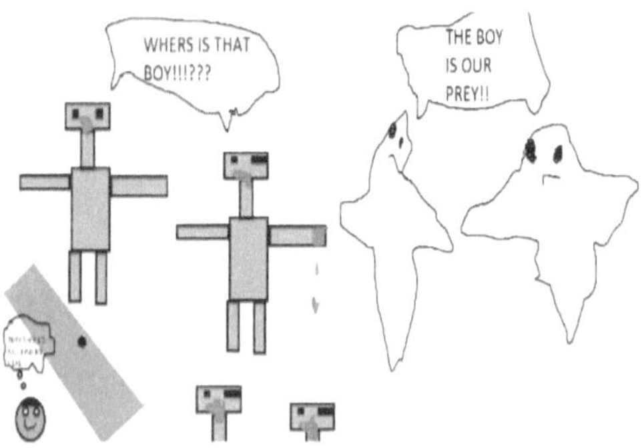

He came out of the door but as he came out, one of the

zombies saw behind and he started to run again but the zombies did not chase him. Now he come to know that the zombie was seeing back and thinking how he escaped from them. He was very tired and was shaking and shivering because he was afraid of zombies and white ghosts.

He leaned against a wall, then the wall started rotating towards the opposite side and at the opposite side there was darkness so he turned on his torch and he saw some old things and found a paper having some maps, gradually he realised these maps are of the haunted house.

From outside the zombies came to know that he is inside the secret room and they started to break the wall. In the old things he found some old maps. He now began to search how to get out with the help of the maps.

He found another way of getting out of the secret room so he casted a spell that was scribbled on another map of the secret room now he got the door to get out so he carried all the maps, he went out he climbed the stairs but as he was getting out, he saw a giant spider it was as big as his palm so he searched for something to get rid of the spider.

And voila! he found some papers scattered all around the floor. He packed bunch of papers, rolled it in a hard rod and hit the spider and the spider ran away and Yohaan started running after the spider, he found the spider hiding behind the broken bookshelf lying in one corner of the room. He gathered all the courage to once again hit the spider and this time it could not escape and the spider fell on the floor lifeless.

Chapter 2 - The Skeletons

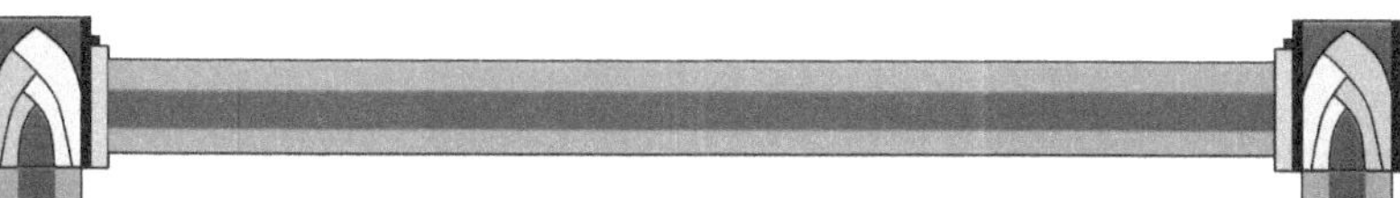

When he came out of the secret room, he found himself in the backyard of the haunted house. He was astonished to see so many graves and was scared at that movement he saw something coming out of the graves and that was skeletons! Now he was trying to act brave he had a wooden sword he tried to fight with the skeletons but they were too many of them and alone he couldn't defeat them but still he fought and one of the skeletons fell into a pond of fishes. Those fishes were scavengers and they jumped to gulp the skeleton. The skeleton

screamed a lot when the fishes tried to swallow him.

The other skeletons panicked and was preparing to shoot arrows at him but Yohaan managed to run away. The skeletons followed him but Yohaan ran and he fell into a big hole then from behind the skeletons began to laugh. Yohaan started finding a map of that trap finally he found one and it was written on it that we have to dig a little bit. So Yohaan started digging with his sword. He found a little tunnel he got inside it and the tunnel came upwards and inside a little room.

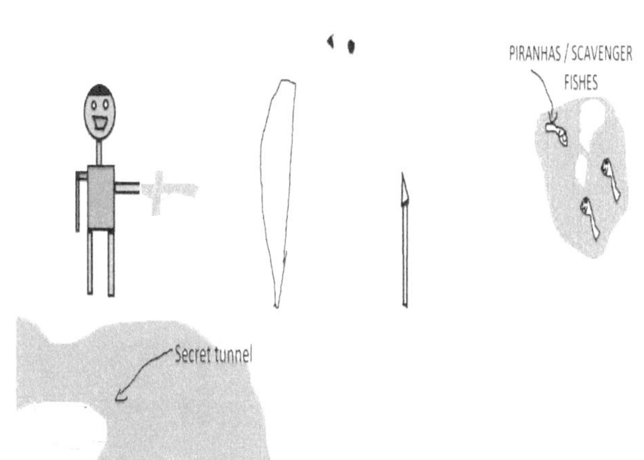

The room was comfortable he relaxed for some time he thought that the skeletons can come through the tunnel so he blocked the tunnel using the items of the room. There was a lamp he switched on the lamp and he saw a work table there was a laptop there he thought that he could communicate to

other people he tried to switch on the laptop but it wasn't a laptop it was a type of GPS!

Yohaan saw that it is the GPS of the haunted house and it is more useful than the maps, he switched on it and it was old but still in use he got to know that the room is opposite to the zombies' room. He searched for anything he could use to protect himself from zombies. He found a sword which had different features it had features like laser sword, torch, gun with the current running fiercely.

Now he was ready to go inside the zombies' room. The zombies' room, door was slightly open he saw inside peeking from the hole the place was very untidy. The zombies were sleeping on their beds. Yohaan got inside the room he was walking quietly and was trying not to make a single noise. But there his torch light came to one zombie's eye and he woke up wondering what came into his eyes.

The zombie shouted and all the zombies woke up. For a moment Yohaan was scared but he took his laser sword and started attacking at the zombies the zombies were weaker than the current of the laser sword. They ran away Yohaan ran behind them then he saw there was a feature of catching zombies in the sword. He caught all the zombies and started to see the GPS.

Chapter 3- Black Ghosts

Yohaan got to know that in the other room there were black ghosts! He went in the room of the black ghosts. The black ghosts knew that Yohaan had trapped the zombies so they were throwing fireballs from their mouth. Yohaan used the laser sword as a gun but the black ghosts still shot the fireballs.

Yohaan also tried to shoot the black ghosts but the gun was not so powerful. Yohaan got out of the room the black ghosts followed him and started to shoot fireballs, Yohaan saw a shield mode on the laser sword before he switched on that button, he takes his backpack on his chest and then he switched on that button suddenly the gun turned into a shield and stuck to Yohaan's back. He can see the features of the laser sword on his left arm. Now he removed his wooden sword from his backpack so he can fight with anyone.

Yohaan ran very fast but the Black Ghosts were faster than him. The shield protected Yohaan from the fireballs as he was searching for a map of that place, he was not getting it so he searched more and more at last he found a map of that place and that was a secret bunker he casted a spell and that was -

"Oh, Bunker Oh Bunker Where Are You Come to Me, I Am Waiting for You"

Then a voice came back and said-

"Come Here Come Here I Am the Bunker No More Waiting for You"

Yohaan got the bunker and ran towards it, there were deep stairs he came down and he saw many shiny things just like priceless jewels on the roof of the bunker and there was a Holy sword just made for Black ghosts, Yohaan took that sword. "Oh Myyyyyyyyyy Gooooooooooooooood"

He was amazed to see those jewels as he took out one of them, a voice came and said –

"What Have You Done Now the Bunker Gate Will Close In 10 Seconds"

Yohaan was shocked he ran fast there was only 5 seconds left, he went out just in the nick of time. He saw the black ghosts coming to him he ran once again this time but he had the Holy sword and he had the shield at his back so he took the shield to his right hand and the Holy sword on his left hand and fought to the black ghosts. The black ghosts were scared of the Holy sword and they couldn't use their fireballs since Yohaan had a shield and that was the end of Black ghosts.

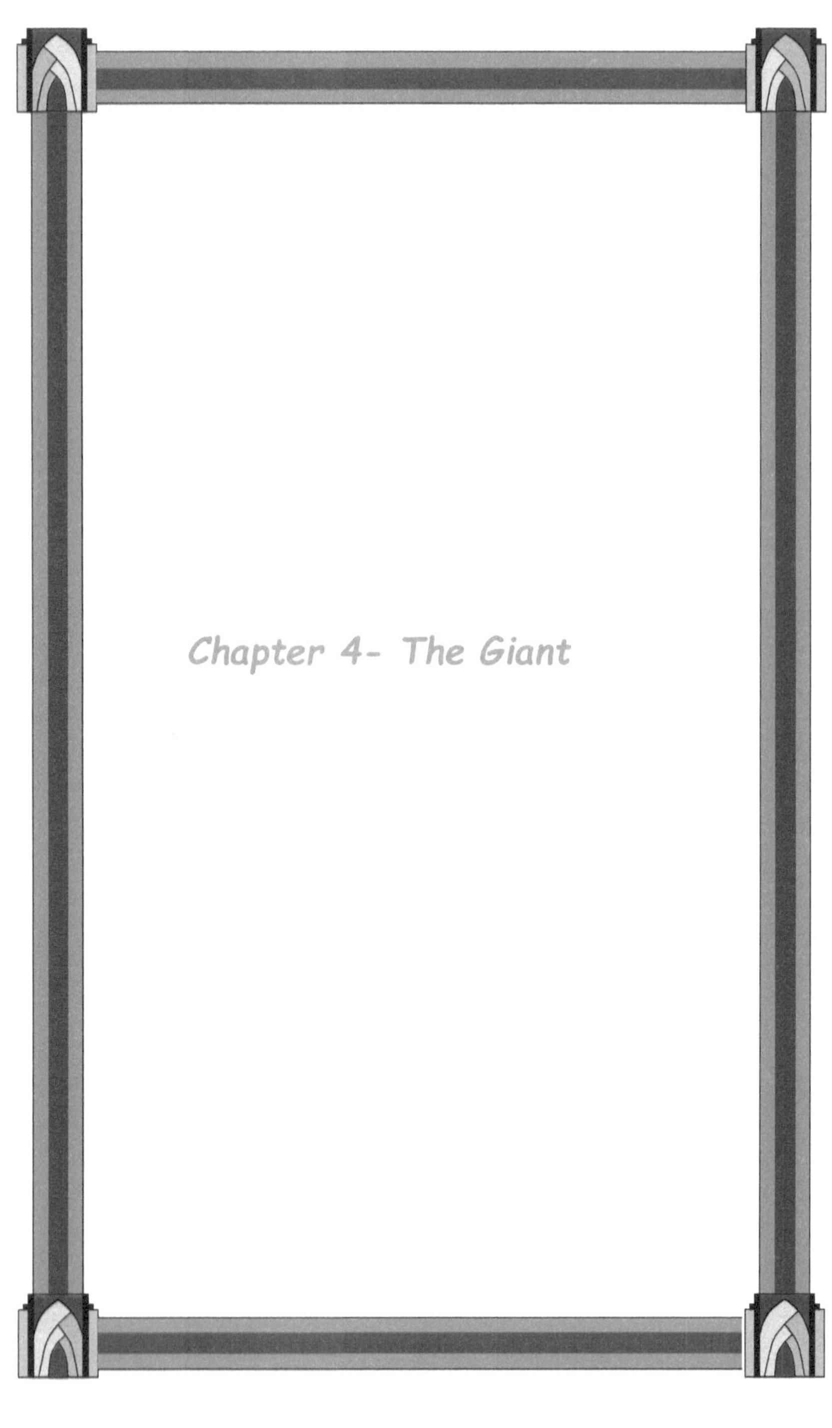

Chapter 4- The Giant

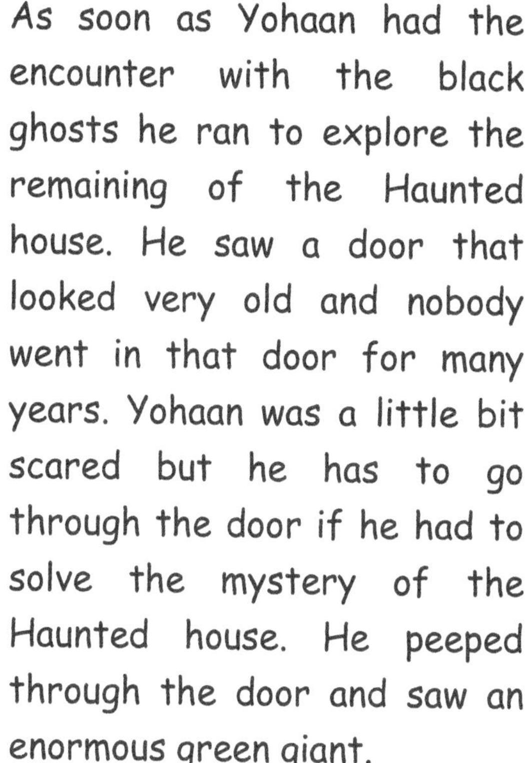

As soon as Yohaan had the encounter with the black ghosts he ran to explore the remaining of the Haunted house. He saw a door that looked very old and nobody went in that door for many years. Yohaan was a little bit scared but he has to go through the door if he had to solve the mystery of the Haunted house. He peeped through the door and saw an enormous green giant.

Yohaan tried to go inside and he went but there was a pebble and by mistake he kicked it. The giant stood up and ran towards him. Yohaan too ran fast and the giant chased him, he knew it was a matter of seconds and the giant will catch him and may gobble him.

Then he remembered that the GPS might have some info about the giant and he switched on the GPS and sure enough he found out that the giant really likes some snacks. But Yohaan has to stop because he has to take the snacks out of the bag but the giant won't let him to do that.

Then Yohaan had a great idea he went to the room of some really spooky creatures and the giant chased him there then Yohaan said to the spooky creatures and the giant that who is better and the spooky creatures and the giant had a great war. Then there Yohaan had the time to pull out the snacks from the bag and by the time the war ended. The giant won and Yohaan gave him a bag of snacks as a prize now the giant was very happy and he became pals with Yohaan.

Now as they both are friends so the giant followed Yohaan in the next room.

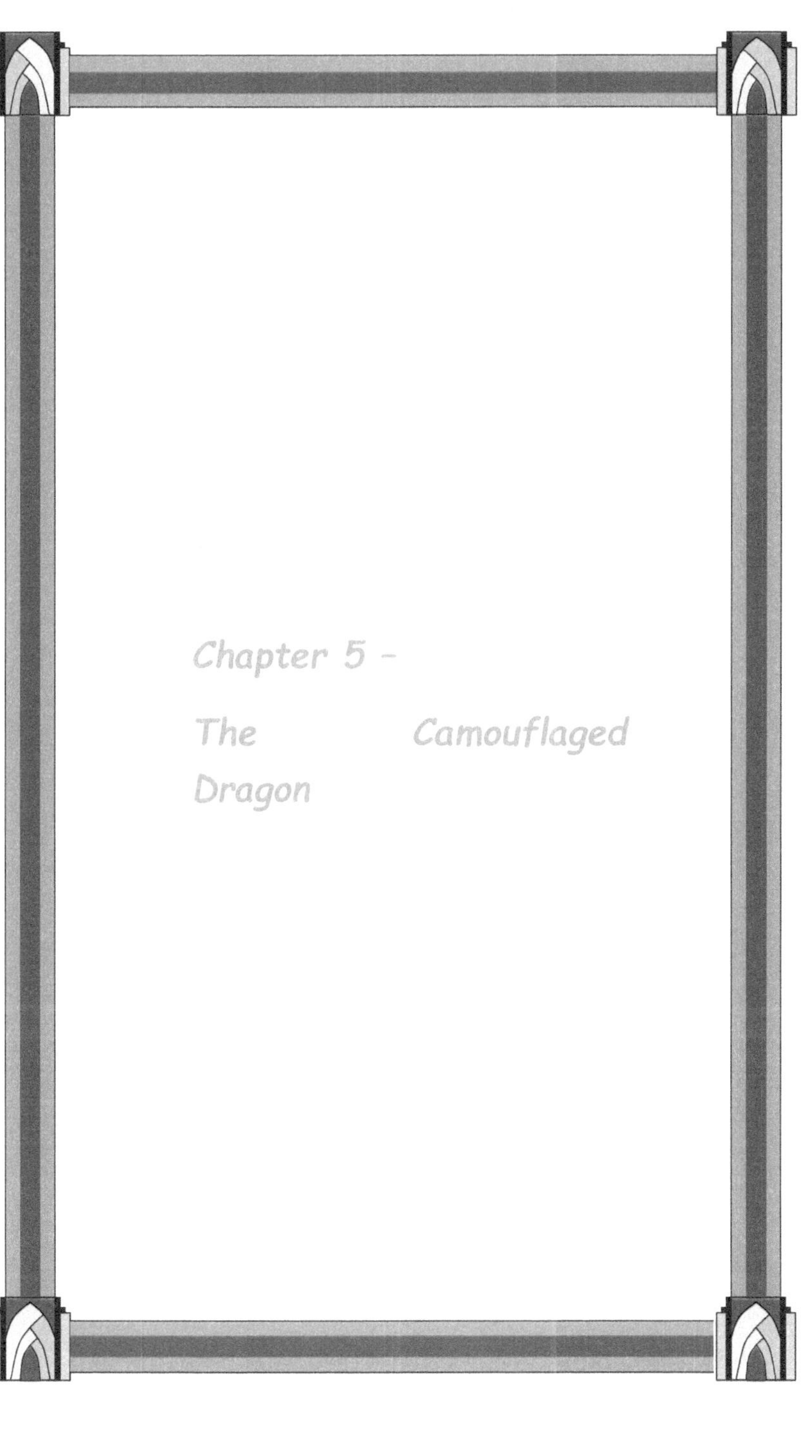

Chapter 5 –
The   Camouflaged
Dragon

Then Yohaan started walking again and he heard some weird noises from behind and the giant was chasing him again Yohaan threw some snacks out of his bag and the giant sat to eat them.

Till then Yohaan was finding out a was how to get rid of the giant. Yohaan saw there was Laser Blaster in the GPS and began to search for it he found it right behind a giant rock. He picked the Laser Blaster up and went where the giant was eating his snacks and he shot at the giant, he fell down and that was the end of the giant.

Now Yohaan was relieved that the giant was not there anymore. He found a place like a cave so he went inside it was pretty dark but he had his torch he thought nothing was there so he was going out of there but as soon as he walked out, he heard a voice and when he turned around to see what it was then he saw a dragon that was camouflaged all the time!

So now Yohaan was scared of the dragon and the dragon stood up and he sneezed but when he sneezed out came fire from his mouth! Yohaan thought the dragon was about to throw the fire on him so he ran but the dragon had wings and he flew all the time but since it was in the house he can't fly and he was not good at running. So Yohaan could run but still the dragons fire had a good range. Now Yohaan was hungry and the dragon was right behind him.

The dragon was boiling with anger and Yohaan was finding a way to fight back to the Dragon. Yohaan saw there was tunnel like thing in the wall front of him and he went inside it and there was light in the tunnel and so bright that Yohaan had to close his eyes.

Then light went and Yohaan saw some kind of rocket

launcher and on it a WARNING was there "YOU CAN FIGHT WITH IT BUT BE CAREFUL". So Yohaan took the launcher with him and rushed out of the tunnel.

When the dragon saw the launcher, he was afraid and it was thinking that how Yohaan found that. So Yohaan took the launcher and shot the rocket on the dragon and Yohaan was staying away because on the launcher it said to be careful now the dragon was dead. Now after so much of running and escaping here he is tired and looking for a scrumptious meal luckily, he grabbed a Paratha from his bag.

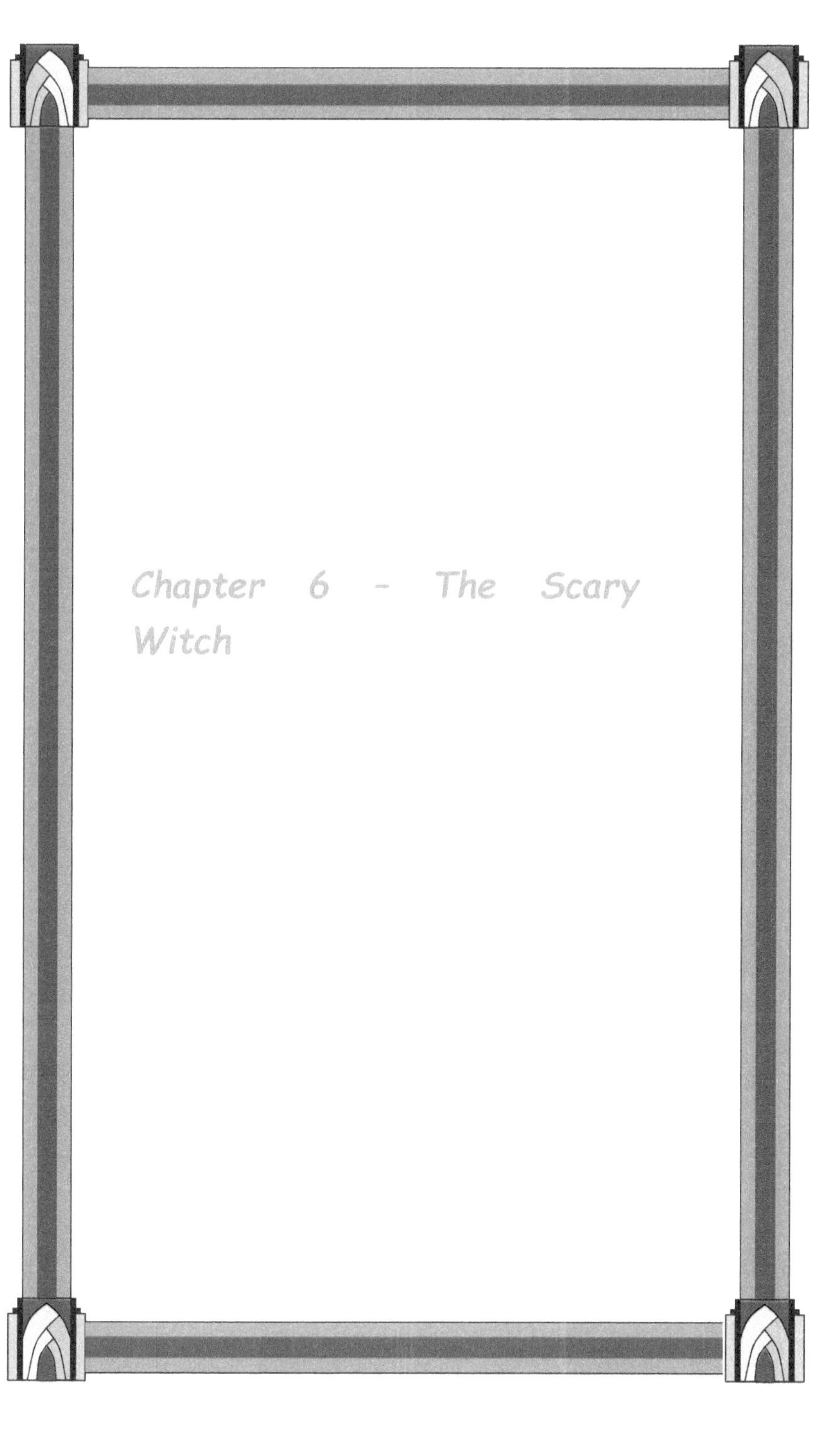

Chapter 6 – The Scary Witch

After the dragon was dead Yohaan started roaming around the haunted house again. Then he heard an evil laugh to his right side and there was a room with a black door so he opened the door a little bit and peeped inside and saw a witch!

Yohaan was really really scared now all the giant, zombie, dragon was ok but the witch is next level with all that black magic and other stuff it was really hard for Yohaan to fight with her. So Yohaan saw that one of the maps was that in one secret room was a magic wand.

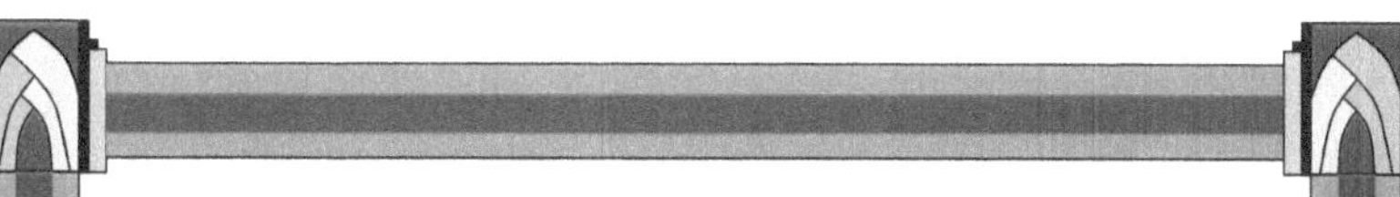

Yohaan went to the witch and tried to cast some spells but only one spell was correct which was to create hundreds of rubber duckies and that was totally useless. The witch casted a spell which created lightning bolts. So Yohaan casted that spell to and one of the lightning bolts almost hit the witch. Then Yohaan ran and he was thinking that soon the witch will catch him and make him an ingredient of a potion or something.

Then a wizard magically appeared and he asked Yohaan what was happening so Yohaan told him what had happened and Yohaan didn't knew that the wizard was a kind person. The wizard was so powerful that the second the witch saw him the witch ran and was trying to escape from the wizard.

The wizard casted a spell and the witch was now transformed to a frog and the wizard kicked her out of the house and to some another place.

Chapter 7 - The Naughty Goblins

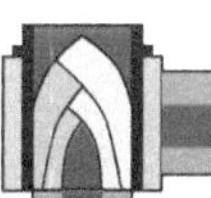

As soon as the witch turned to a frog Yohaan went to find the last monster. There was a room that was old and rusty Yohaan opened the door and saw a bunch of goblins! The goblins like to irritate people and mostly kids as Yohaan was alone so they tried to pounce on Yohaan.

Yohaan reached to his bag and threw an action figure on them the goblins thought that it was real person so when the broke it they came to know that wasn't a real person and the action figure gave Yohaan the time he needed to run away.

The goblins didn't know where Yohaan went so they separated in groups of two to find Yohaan. Some went to the zombie's room; some went to the black ghost's room and to every room! They were pretty shocked to see that Yohaan had defeated every single monster. They met to each other were they stayed and discussed every goblin said that they couldn't find Yohaan. But they didn't check their own room.

Yohaan didn't knew the formula to defeat the goblins so he stayed in the room all night and when it was morning an idea flashed to his brain.

Yohaan went to the goblins and the goblins chased Yohaan. Yohaan climbed the tunnel and the goblins too but something happened that took the goblins' living daylights out when the sun was on their head the goblins screamed and turned to stone statue! This way Yohaan came out of the house and all the monsters were defeated so from then onwards no one was scared to go there and all the people cheered to Yohaan.

Hip   Hip   Hooray!   Hip   Hip
Hooray! Hip Hip Hooray....

It was a happy end.

THE END